Reprint Publishing

FOR PEOPLE WHO GO FOR ORIGINALS.

www.reprintpublishing.com

ALICE IN BLUNDERLAND

Alice in
Blunderland

An Iridescent Dream

By
JOHN KENDRICK BANGS

Illustrated by
ALBERT LEVERING

New York
Doubleday, Page & Company
1907

CONTENTS

ILLUSTRATIONS

ALICE IN BLUNDERLAND

viii

ALICE IN BLUNDERLAND

CHAPTER I

IT WAS one of those dull, drab, de-
pressing days when somehow or
other it seemed as if there wasn't anything anywhere for anybody to do. It
was raining outdoors, so that Alice could
not amuse herself in the garden, or call
upon her friend Little Lord Fauntleroy
up the street; and downstairs her mother
was giving a Bridge Party for the benefit
of the M. O. Hot Tamale Company, which
had lately fallen upon evil days. Alice's
mother was a very charitably disposed
person, and while she loathed gambling
in all its forms, was nevertheless willing
for the sake of a good cause to forego her
principles on alternate Thursdays, but
she was very particular that her little
daughter should be kept aloof from

contaminating influences, so that Alice found herself locked in the nursery and, as I have already intimated, with nothing to do. She had read all her books—The House of Mirth, the novels of Hall Caine and Marie Corelli—the operation for appendicitis upon her dollie, while very successful indeed, had left poor Flaxilocks without a scrap of sawdust in her veins, and therefore unable to play; and worst of all, her pet kitten, under the new city law making all felines public property, had grown into a regular cat and appeared only at mealtimes, and then in so disreputable a condition that he was not thought to be fit company for a child of seven.

"Oh dear!" cried Alice impatiently, as she sat rocking in her chair, listening to the pattering of the rain upon the roof of the veranda. "I do wish there was something to do, or somebody to do, or somewhere to go. The Gov'ment ought to provide covered playgrounds for children on wet days.   It wouldn't cost much to put a glass cover on the Park!"

"A very good idea! I'll make a note of that," said a squeaky little voice at her side.

Alice sprang to her feet in surprise. She had supposed she was alone, and for a moment she was frightened, but a glance around reassured her, for strange to say, seated on the radiator warming his toes was her old friend the Hatter, the queer old chap she had met in her marvellous trip through Wonderland, and with him was the March Hare, the Cheshire Cat, and the White Knight from Looking Glass Land.

THE CHESHIRE CAT

"Why—you dear old things!" she cried. "You here?"

"I don't know about these others, but I'm here," returned the Hatter. "The others seem to be here, but I respectfully decline to take my solemn daffydavy on the subject, because my doctor says I'm all the time seeing things that ain't. Besides I don't believe in swearing."

"We're here all right," put in the March Hare. "I know because we ain't anywhere else, and when you ain't anywhere else you can make up your mind that you're here."

THE MARCH HARE

"Well, I'm awfully glad to see you," said Alice. "I've been so lonesome——"

"We know that," said the White Knight. "We've been studying your case lately and we thought we'd come down and see what we could do for you. The fact is the Hatter here has founded a model city, where everything goes just right, and we came to ask you to pay us a call."

"A city?" cried Alice.

"Yep," said the March Hare.   "It's called Blunderland and between you and me I don't believe anybody but the Hatter could have invented one like it. His geegantic brain conceived the whole thing, and I tell you it's a corker."

"Where is it?" asked Alice.

"That's telling," said the Hatter. "I haven't had it copyrighted yet, and until I do I ain't going to tell where it is. You can't be too careful about property these days with copperations lurkin' around everywhere to grab everything in sight."

"LISTEN HERE"

"What's a copperation?" asked Alice.

"What? Never heard of a Coppera-tion?" demanded the Hatter. "Mercy! Ever hear of the Mumps, or the Measles, or the Whooping Cough?"

"Yes—but I never knew they were called Copperations," said Alice.

"Well, they ain't, but they're no worse —so they ought to be," said the Hatter. "Listen here. I'll tell you what a cop-peration is."

And putting his hat in front of his mouth like a telephone the Hatter recited the following poem through it:

THE COPPERATION

A copperation is a beast
　　With forty leven paws
That doesn't ever pay the least
　　Attention to the laws.

It grabs whatever comes in sight
　　From hansom cabs to socks
And with a grin of mad delight
　　It turns 'em into stocks

And then it takes a rubber hose
  Connected with the sea
And pumps 'em full of H_2Os
  Of various degree

And when they're swollen up so stout
  You'd think they'd surely bust
They souse 'em once again and out
  They come at last a Trust

And when the Trust is ready for
  One last and final whack
They let the public in the door
  To buy the water back.

"See?" said the Hatter as he finished.

"No," said Alice. "It sounded very pretty through your hat, but I don't understand it. Why should people buy water when they can get it for nothing in the ocean?"

"You're like all the rest," groaned the Hatter. "Nobody seems to understand but me, and somehow or other I can't make it clear to other people."

"You might if you didn't talk through

your hat," grinned the Cheshire Cat.

"Then I'd have to stop being a public character," said the Hatter. "I'm not going to sacrifice my career just because you're too ignorant to see what I'm driving at. I don't mind telling you though, Alice, that outside of poetry a Copperation is a Creature devised by Selfish Interests to secure the Free Coinage of the Atlantic Ocean."

"Little drops of water,
    Plenty of hot air,
Make a Copperation
    A pretty fat affair,"

warbled the March Hare.

"O well," said Alice, "what about it? Suppose there is such an animal around. What are we going to do about it?"

"We're going to gerraple with it," said the Hatter, with a valiant shake of his hat. "We're going to grab it by its throat, and shake it down, and shackle it so that in forty years it will become as

tame as a fly or any other highly domes-
ticated animal."

"But how?" asked Alice. "You
aren't going to
do this yourself,
are you? Single
h a n d e d a n d
alone?"

"Y e s," said
the Hatter.
"The March Hare
and the White
K n i g h t a n d I.
We've started
a city to do it
with. We've
sprinkled our
streets with

THE MUNICIPAL CHEWERY

Rough on Copperations until there isn't
one left in the place. Everything in town
belongs to the People—street cars, gut-
ters, pavements, theatres, electric light,
cabs, manicures, dogs, cats, canary birds,
hotels, barber shops, candy stores, hats,

umbrellas, bakeries, cakeries, steakeries, shops,—you can't think of a thing that the city don't own.   No more private ownership of anything from a toothbrush to a yacht, and the result is we are all happy."

"It sounds fine," said Alice. "Though I think I should rather own my own toothbrush."

"You naturally would under the old system," assented the Hatter. "Under a system of private ownership owning your own teeth you'd prefer to own your own toothbrush, but our Council has just passed a law making teeth public property. You see we found that some people had teeth and other people hadn't, which is hardly a fair condition under a Republican form of Government. It gave one class of citizens a distinct advantage over other people and the Declaration of Independence demands absolute equality for all. One man owning his own teeth could eat all the hickory nuts he wanted just because he had teeth to crack 'em with, while another man not having teeth had either to swallow 'em whole, which ruined his digestion, or go without, which wasn't fair."

"I see," said Alice.

"So it occurred to Mr. Alderman

THE MUNICIPAL TOOTHERY

March Hare here," continued the Hatter, "that we should legislate in the matter, and at our last session we passed a law providing for the Municipal Ownership of Teeth, so that now when a toothless wanderer wants a hickory nut cracked he has a perfectly legal right to stop anybody in the street who has teeth and make him crack the nut for him. Of course we've had a little trouble enforcing the law—alleged private rights are always difficult to get around. Long-continued possession has seemed so to convince people that they have inherent rights to the things they have enjoyed that they put up a fight and appeal to the Constitution and all that, and even when you mention the fact, as I did in a case that came up the other day (when a man refused to bite off another chap's cigar for him), that the Constitution doesn't mention teeth anywhere in all its classes, they are not easy to convince. This fellow insisted that his teeth were private property, and no city law should make them public property. He's going to take it to the Supreme Court. Meanwhile his teeth are in the custody of the sheriff.''

"And what has become of the man?" asked Alice.

"He's in the custody of the sheriff too," said the Hatter. "We couldn't arrange it any other way except by pulling his teeth, and he didn't want that."

"I can't blame him," said Alice reflectively. "I should hate to have my teeth taken away from me."

"O there's no obfuscation about it," said the Hatter.

"Confuscation," corrected the March Hare. "I wish you would get that word right. It's too important to fool with."

"Thank you," replied the Hatter. "My mind is on higher things than mere words. However, as I was saying, there is no cobfuscation about it. We don't take a man's teeth away from him without compensation. We pay him what the teeth are worth and place them at the service of the whole community."

"Where do you get the money to pay him?" asked Alice.

"We give him a Municipal Bond," explained the Hatter. "It's a ten per cent. bond costing two cents to print. When he cracks a hickory nut for the public, the man he cracks it for pays him a cent. He rings this up on a cash register he carries pinned to his vest, and at the end of every week turns in the cash to the City Treasury. That money is used to pay the interest on the bonds. The scheme has the additional advantage that it makes a man's teeth negotiable property in the sense that whereas under the old system he couldn't very well sell his teeth, under the new system he can sell the bond if he gets hard up. Moreover, the City Government having acquired control has to pay all his dentist's bills, supply tooth powder and so on, which results in a great saving to the individual. It hardly costs the city anything, except for the Tooth Inspector, who is paid $1,200 a year, but we can handle that easily enough, provided the people will use the Public Teeth in sufficiently large numbers to bring in dividends. Anyhow, we have gone in for it, and I see no reason why it should not work as well as any other Municipal Ownership scheme."

"I should love to go and see your city," said

"HANDING HER A CARD"

Alice, who, though not quite convinced as to the desirability of the Municipal Ownership of Teeth, was nevertheless very much interested.

"Very well," said the Hatter. "We can go at once, for I see the train is already standing in the Station."

"The Station?" cried Alice. "What Station?"

But before the Hatter could answer, Alice, glancing through the window, caught sight of a very beautiful train standing before the veranda, and in a moment she found herself stepping on board with her friends, while a soft-spoken guard at the door was handing her an engraved card upon a silver salver "Respectfully Inviting Miss Alice to Step Lively There."

CHAPTER II

THE IMMOVABLE TROLLEY

"WHAT an extraordinary car," said Alice, as she stepped into the brilliantly lighted vehicle. "It doesn't seem to have any end to it," she added as she passed down the aisle, looking for the front platform.

"It hasn't," said the Hatter. "It just runs on forever."

"Doesn't it stop anywhere?" cried Alice in amazement.

"It stops everywhere," said the Hatter. "What I mean is it hasn't any ends at all. It's just one big circular car that runs all around the city and joins itself where it began in the beginning. We call it the M. O. Express, M. O. standing for Municipal Ownership——"

"And Money Owed," laughed a

Weasel that sat on the other side of the car.

"Put that fellow off," said the March Hare indignantly. "Conductor—out with him."

"PUT THAT FELLOW OFF"

The Conductor immediately threw the Weasel out of the window, as ordered, and the Hatter resumed.

"We call it the express because it is so fast," he continued.

"You'd hardly think it was going at all, observed Alice, as she noticed the entire lack of motion in the car.

"It isn't," said the Hatter. "It's built on a solid foundation and doesn't move an inch, and yet at the same time it runs all around the city. It was *my* idea," he added proudly.

"But you said it was fast," protested Alice.

"And so it is, my child," said the Hatter kindly. "It's as fast as though it was glued down with mucilage. There's several ways of being fast, you know. Did you ever hear of the Ballade of the *Nancy P. D. Q.?*"

"No," said Alice.

"It's a Sea Song in B flat," said the Hatter. "I will sing it for you."

And placing his hat before his lips to give a greater mellowness to his voice, the Hatter sang:

THE BALLADE OF THE *NANCY P. D. Q.*

O the good ship *Nancy P. D. Q.*
From up in Boston, Mass.,
Went sailing o'er the bounding blue
Cargoed with apple sass.

She sailed around Ogunkit Bay
  Down past the Banks of Quogue,
And on a brilliant summer's day,
Just off the coast of Mandelay,
  She landed in a fog.

So brace the topsails close, my lads,
  And stow your grog, my crew,
For the waves are steep and the fog is deep
  Round the *Nancy P. D. Q.*

As in the fog she groped around—
  The night was black as soot—
She ran against Long Island Sound,
  Out where the codfish toot.
And when the moon rose o'er the scene
  So smiling, sweet and bland,
She poked her nose so sharp and keen—
'Twas freshly painted olive green—
  Deep in a bar of sand.

So splice the garboard strakes, my lads,
  And reef the starboard screw—
For it sticks like tar, that sandy bar,
  To the *Nancy P. D. Q.*

O the Skipper swore with a "Yeave-ho-ho!"
  And the crew replied "Hi-hi!"
And then, with a cheerful "Heave-ho-yo,"
  They pumped the bowsprit dry.
"Three cheers!" the Mate cried with a sneeze
  "Hurrah for this old boat!
She sails two knots before the breeze,
But on the bar, by Jingo, she's
  The fastest thing afloat!"

So up with the gallant flag, my lads,
  With a hip-hip-hip-hooroo,
For the liner fast is now outclassed
  By the *Nancy P. D. Q.*

Alice scratched her chin in perplexity, but the Hatter never stopped.

"I got an idea from that ballad," he rattled on. "If you want trains fast you've got to build 'em fast."

"Yes, but if they don't go—how does anybody get anywhere?" asked Alice.

"They can get off and walk," said the Hatter. "And it's a great deal less dangerous getting off a train that doesn't move than off one that does."

"I can see that," said Alice. "That weasel, for instance, would have been badly hurt if he had been thrown through the window of a moving car."

"REQUESTED THE HATTER TO CRACK A FILBERT FOR HIM"

"That's it exactly," said the Hatter. "As Alderman March Hare puts it, we M. O. people are after the comfort and safety of the people first, last and all the

time. Everything else is a tertiary con-
sideration merely."

"What's tertiary?" asked Alice.

"Third," said the Hatter. "To come
in third. It's a combination of turtle
and dromedary."

Just at this moment a man walking
through the car stopped and requested
the Hatter to crack a filbert for him,
which the Hatter cheerfully did. The
passer-by thanked him and paid him a
cent, which the Hatter immediately rang
up on a small cash register on his vest,
as required by the laws of Blunderland.

"That's the way the Municipal Ownership of Teeth works," said the Hatter as
the man passed on, and then he resumed.
"This street railway business, however,
was a much harder proposition than the
Municipal Ownership of Teeth. When
we took the railways over of course we
had to run 'em on the old system until
we'd learned the business. The first
thing we did was to get educated men for

Motormen and Conductors—polite fellows, you know, who'd stop a car when you asked 'em to, and when they started wouldn't do it with such a jerk that in nine cases out of ten it was only the back door that kept the car from being yanked clean from under your feet, letting you land in the street behind."

"I know," said Alice. "Like a game of snap the whip."

"Exactly," said the Hatter. "Under the old method of starting a car you never knew, when you were going home nights, whether you'd land in the bosom of your family or in a basket of eggs somebody was bringing home from market. So we advertised for polite motormen and conductors, and we got a great lot of them, mostly retired druggists, floor-walkers, poets and fellows like that, with a few ex-politicians thrown in to give tone to the service, and we put them on, but they didn't know anything about motoring, unfortunately. Somehow or other good manners and expert motoring didn't seem to go together, and in consequence we had a fearful lot of collisions at first. I don't think there was a whole back

"BANGED INTO THE CAR AHEAD"

platform in the outfit at the end of the week, no matter which way the car was going."

"Must have been awful," said Alice.

"It was," said the Hatter, "and the public began to complain. One man who

got his nose pinched between two cars
sued us for damages and we had to return
his fare.   Finally one day one of the old
bobtail cars got running away, and the
first we knew it banged into the car ahead
and went right through it, coming out
in front still going like mad after the next
car, and we knew something had to be
done."

"Mercy!" cried Alice.   "I should
think the passengers in the first car would
have sued you for that."

"They would have," said the Hatter,
"if they could have scraped enough of
themselves together again to appear in
court."

"It was a hard problem," said the
March Hare.

"The hardest ever," asserted the
Hatter.   "But the White Knight there
gave me a clue to the solution—he's our
Copperation Council—and I put it up
to him for an opinion, and after thinking
it over for two months he reported.   The

only way to prevent collisions, said he, is to cut the ends off the cars. That was it, wasnt' it, Judge?" he added, turning to the White Knight.

"Yes," said the Knight, "only I put it in poetry. My precise words were

> The only way that I can find
>> To stop this car colliding stunt
> Is cutting off the end behind
>> And likewise that in front."

"Splendid!" cried Alice, clapping her hands in glee. "That's fine."

"Thank you," said the White Knight. "You see, Miss Alice, I made a personal study of collisions. The Mayor here ordered a fresh one every day for me to investigate, and I noticed that whenever two cars bunked into each other it was always at the ends and never in the middle. The conclusion was inevitable. The ends being the venerable spot, abolish them."

"A very careful and conscientious

"THE CHIEF ENGINEER"

public servant," whispered the March Hare aside to Alice. "When we have Municipal Ownership of the Federal Government we're going to put him on the Supreme Court Bench. He means vulnerable when he says venerable, but you mustn't mind that. When we have Municipal Ownership of the English Language we'll make the words mean what we want 'em to."

"Then of course the question arose as to how we could do this," said the Hatter. "I got the Chief Engineer of our Department of Public Works to make some experiments, and would you believe it, when we cut the ends off the cars, there were still other ends left? No matter how far we clipped 'em, it was the same. It's a curious scientific fact that you can't cut off the end of anything and leave it endless. We tried it with a lot of things—cars, lengths of hose, coils of wire, rope—everything we could think of—always with the same result. Ends were endless, but nothing else was. As a matter of fact they multiplied on us. One car that had two ends when we began was cut in the middle, and then was found to have four ends instead of two."

"That's so, isn't it!" cried Alice,

"IT CAME TO ME LIKE A FLASH"

"It unquestionably is," said the Hatter, "and we were at our wits' ends until one night it came to me like a flash. I had gone to bed on a Park Bench, according to my custom of using nothing that is not owned by the city, for I am very serious about this thing, when just as I was dozing off the whole scheme unfolded itself. Build a circular car, of course. One big enough to go all around the city. That would solve so many problems. With only one car, there'd be no car ahead, which always irritates people who miss it and then have to take it later. With only one car, there could be no collisions. With only one car we could get along with only one motorman and one conductor at a time, thus giving the others time to go to dancing school and learn good manners. With only one car, and that a permanent fixture, nobody could miss it. If it didn't move we could economise on motive power, and even bounce the motorman without injury to the service, if he should happen to be impudent to the Board of Aldermen; nobody would be run over by it; nobody would be injured getting on and off; it wouldn't make any difference if the motorman didn't see the passenger who wanted to get aboard. Being circular there'd always be room enough to go around, and there'd be no front or back platform for the people to stand on or get thrown off of going round the curves. The expenses of keeping up the roadbed would be nothing, because, being motionless, the car wouldn't jolt even if it ran over a thank-you-marm a mile high, and best of all, a circular car has no ends to collide with other ends, which makes it absolutely safe. I never heard of a car colliding with itself, did you?"

"No, I never did," replied Alice.

"Nor I neither," said the March Hare. "I don't think it ever happened, and therefore I reason that it ain't going to happen."

"And how do the people like it?" asked Alice.

"O, they're getting to like it," replied the Hatter. "At first they didn't want to ride on the thing at all. They said what you did, that they didn't seem to be getting anywhere, and they hated to walk home, but after awhile we proved to them that walking was a very healthful exercise, and on rainy nights they found the covered car a good deal of a convenience, especially when under the old system of private ownership of umbrellas they had left their bumbershoots at home. Once or twice they lost their tempers and sassed the conductor, but he put them in jail for lazy majesty—a German disease that we have imported for the purpose. As an officer of the Government the conductor has a right to arrest anybody who sasses him as guilty of sedition, and a night or two in jail takes the fun out of that."

"Have you had any elections since

you established it?" asked Alice, whose father had once run for Mayor, and who therefore knew something about politics.

"No," said the Hatter with an easy laugh. "But we will have one in the spring. We shall be reëlected all right."

"How do you know?" asked Alice. "If the people don't like Municipal Ownership——"

"O, but they do," said the March Hare. "You see, Miss Alice, we have employed a safe majority of the voters in the various Departments of our M. O. system, their terms expiring coincidentally with our own—so if they vote against us they vote against themselves. It really makes Municipal Ownership self-perpetrating."

"He means perpetuating," whispered the March Hare.

"Ah," said Alice. "I see."

Just then a heavy gong like a huge fire alarm sounded and all the passengers sprang to their feet and made for the doors.

"What's that?" cried Alice, timidly, as she rose up hurriedly with all the rest.

"Don't be alarmed. It's only the signal that our time is up," said the Hatter. "We must get out now and make room for others who may wish to use the cars. Nobody can monopolise anything under our system. I will now take you to see our Gas and Hot Air Plant. It is one of the seven wonders of the world."

And the little party descended into the street.

CHAPTER III

THE AROMATIC GAS PLANT

AFTER the little party had descended from the marvellous trolley, concerning which the March Hare observed, most properly, that under private ownership nothing so safe and sane would ever have been thought of, they walked along a beautiful highway, bordered with rosebushes, oleanders and geraniums, until they came to a lovely little park at the entrance to which was a huge sign announcing that within was

THE BLUNDERLAND GAS PLANT.

To tell the truth Alice had not cared particularly to visit the Gas Works, because she had once been driven through what was known at home as the Gas-House district on her way to the ferry,

and her recollections of it were not altogether pleasant. As she recalled it it
was in a rather squalid neighbourhood,
and the odours emanating from it were
not pleasing to what she called her ''oil-
factories.'' But here in Blunderland all
was different. Instead of the huge ugly
retorts rising up out of the ground, sur-
rounded by a quality of air that one could
not breathe with comfort, was as beautiful
a garden as anyone could wish to wander
through, and at its centre there stood a
retort, but not one that looked like a
great iron skull cap painted red. On
the contrary the Municipally Owned
retort had architecturally all the classic
beauty of a Carnegie Library.

"We call it the Retort Courteous,"
said the Hatter pridefully as he gazed at
the structure, and smiled happily as he
noted Alice's very evident admiration
for it. "You see, in urban affairs, as a
mere matter of fitness, we believe in
cultivating urbanity, my child, and in

consequence everything we do is conceived in a spirit of courtesy. The gashouses under private ownership have not been what you would call polite. They were almost invariably heavy, rude, staring structures that reared themselves offensively in the public eye, and our first effort was to subliminate——"

"Ee-liminate," whispered the March Hare.

"I beg your pardon, Mr. Hare," retorted the Hatter. "I did not mean ee-liminate, which means to suppress, but subliminate, which means to sublimify or make sublime. I guess I know my own language."

"Excuse me," said the March Hare meekly. "I haven't studied the M. O. Dictionary beyond the letter Q, Mr. Mayor, and I was not aware that the Common Council had as yet passed favourably upon subliminate, either," he added with some feeling.

"That is because it was not until

yesterday that the Copperation Council decided that subliminate was a constitutional word," said the Hatter sharply. "In view of his report to me, which I wrote myself and therefore know the provisions of, he states that subliminate is a perfectly just and proper word involving no infringement upon the rights of others, and in no wise impairing the value of innocent vested interests, and is therefore legal. Therefore, I shall use it whether the Common Council approves it or not. If they resolve that it is not a good word, I shall veto the resolution. If you don't like it I'll send you your resignation."

"That being the case," said the March Hare, "I withdraw my objections."

"Which," observed the Hatter triumphantly, turning to Alice, "shows you, my dear young lady, the very great value of the Municipal Ownership idea as applied to the Board of Aldermen. As the White Knight put it in one of his

poetical reports printed in Volume 347,
of the Copperation Council's Opinions
for October, 1906, page 926,

> A City may not own its Gas,
>   Its Barber Shops, or Cars
> It may not raise Asparagrass,
>   Or run Official Bars;
> It may not own a big Hotel
>   Or keep a Public Hen,
> But it will always find it well
>   To own its Aldermen.

When Aldermen were owned by private
interests the public interests suffered, but
in this town where the City Fathers belong to the City they have to do what
the City tells them to, or get out."

It sounds good," was all that Alice
could think of to say.

"What I was trying to tell you when
the Alderman interpolated—" the Hatter went on.

"There he goes again!" growled the
March Hare.

"Was that the first thing we did when we took over the Gas Plant was to sublimify the externals of the works along lines of Architectural and Olfactoreal beauty both to the eye and to the nose, two organs of the human structure that private interests seldom pay much attention to. I asked myself two questions. First, is it necessary for a gas works to be ugly? Second, is it necessary for gas works to be so odourwhifferous that the smell of the Automobile is a dream of fragrant beauty alongside of it? To both these questions the answer was plain. Of course it ain't. Beauty can be applied to the lines of a gas-tank just as readily as to the lines of a hippopotamus, and as for the odours, they are due to the fact that gas as it is now made does not smell pleasantly, but there is no reason why it should not be so manufactured that people would be willing to use it on their handkerchiefs. I learned that Professor Burbank of California had developed a cactus plant that could be used for a sofa cushion—why, I asked myself, could he not develop a gas-plant that will put forth flowers the perfume of which should make that of the violet, and the rose, sink into inoculated desoupitude?"

"It hardly seems possible, does it?" said Alice.

"To a private mind it presents insuperable difficulties," said the Hatter, "but to a public mind like my own nothing is impossible. If a man can do a seemingly impossible thing with one plant there is no reason why he shouldn't do a seemingly impossible thing with another plant, so I immediately wrote to Professor Burbank offering him a hundred thousand dollars in Blunderland Deferred Debenture Gas Improvement Bonds a year to come here and see what he could do to transmogrify our gas-plant."

"Oh, I am so glad," cried Alice delightedly. "I should so love to meet

Mr. Burbank and thank him for inventing the coreless apple―――"

"You don't means the Corliss Engine, do you?" asked the White Knight.

"Well, I'm sorry," said the Hatter, "but Mr. Burbank wouldn't come unless we'd pay him real money, which, although we don't publish the fact broadcast, is not in strict accord with the highest principles of Municipal Ownership. We contend that when people work for the common weal they ought to be satisfied to receive their pay in the common wealth, and under the M. O. system the most common kind of wealth is represented by Bonds. Consequently we wrote again to Mr. Burbank, and expressed our regret that a man of his genius should care more for his own selfish interests than for the public weal, and as a sort of sarcasm on his meanness I enclosed five of our 2963 Guaranteed Extension four per cents to pay for the two-cent stamp he had put upon his letter."

"What are the 2963 Guaranteed Extension four per cents?" asked Alice.

They are sinking fund bonds payable in 2963, only we guarantee to extend the date of payment to 3963 in case the sink-

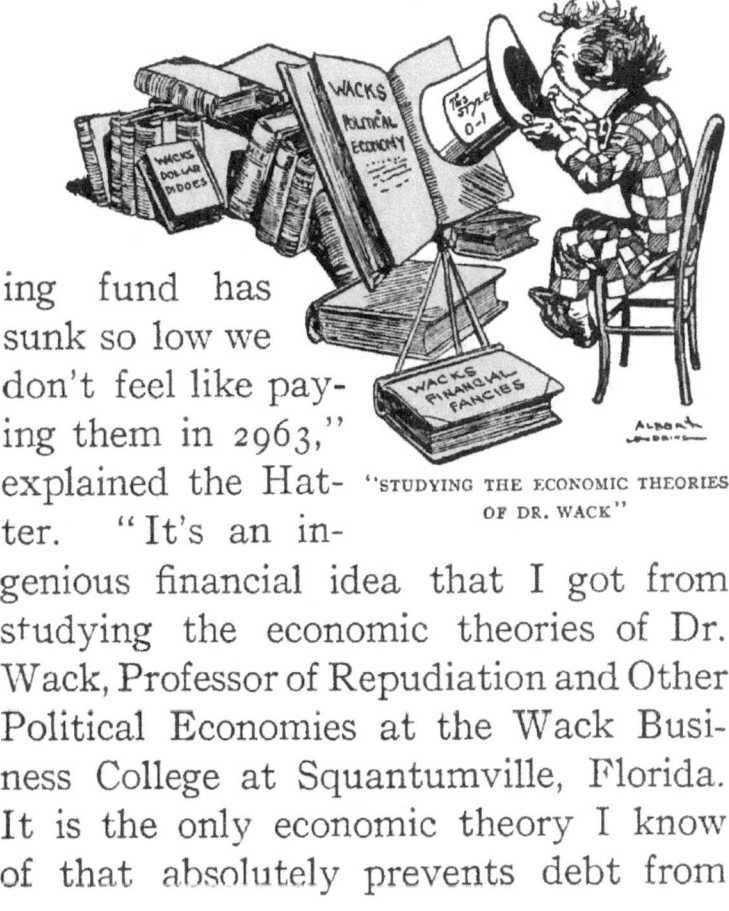

ing fund has sunk so low we don't feel like paying them in 2963," explained the Hatter. "It's an in-

"STUDYING THE ECONOMIC THEORIES OF DR. WACK"

genious financial idea that I got from studying the economic theories of Dr. Wack, Professor of Repudiation and Other Political Economies at the Wack Business College at Squantumville, Florida. It is the only economic theory I know of that absolutely prevents debt from becoming a burden.   But that aside, when Mr. Burbank showed that he preferred fooling with such futile things as pine-apples and hollyhocks, to the really up-lifting work of providing the people with gas that was redolent of the spices of Araby, I resolved to do the thing myself.''

" He is a man of real inventive genius,'' said the March Hare, anxious, apparently, to square himself with the Hatter again.

"Thank you, Alderman,'' said the Hatter.   "It is a real pleasure to find myself strictly in accord with your views once more.   But to resume, Miss Alice— as I say I resolved to tackle the problem myself.''

"Fine,'' said Alice.   "So you went in and studied how to make gas the old way and   then——''

"Not at all,'' interrupted the Hatter. " Not at all.   That would have been fatal. I found that everybody who knew how to make gas the old way said the thing was impossible.   Hence, I reasoned, the man who will find it possible must be somebody who never knew anything about the old way of making gas, and nobody in the whole world knew less about it than I. Manifestly then I became the chosen instrument to work the reform, so I plunged in and you really can't imagine how easy it all turned out. I had no old prejudices in gas-making to overcome, no set, finicky ideas to serve as obstacles to progress, and inside of a week I had it. I filled the gas tanks half full of cologne, and then pumped hot air through them until they were chock full. I figured it out that cologne was nothing more than alcohol flavoured with axiomatic oils——"

"Aromatic," interrupted the March Hare, forgetting himself for the moment.

The Hatter frowned heavily upon the Alderman, and there is no telling what would have happened had not the White Knight interfered to protect the offender.

"It's still an open question, Mr.

Mayor," he observed, " if axiomatic applied to a scent is constitutional. If an odour should become axiomatic we could never get rid of it you see, and I think the Alderman has distinguished authority for his correction, which——"

"THE WHITE KNIGHT INTERFERED"

"O very well," said the Hatter. "Let it go. I prefer axiomatic, but the private predilections of an official should not be permitted to influence his official actions. I intend always to operate within the limits of the law, so if the law says aromatic, aromatic be it. I figured that cologne was nothing more than alcohol flavoured with aromatic oils, and that inasmuch as both alcohol and oil burn readily, there was no reason why hot air passed through them should not burn also, and carry off some of the aroma as well."

"It certainly was a very pretty idea," said Alice.

"All the M. O. ideas are pretty," said the March Hare. "It is only the question of reducing beauty to the basis of practical utility that confronts us."

"And how did it work?" asked Alice, very much interested.

"Beautifully," said the Hatter. "Only it wouldn't burn—just why I haven't been able to find out. But in the matter of perfume it was fine. People who turned on their jets the first night soon found their houses smelling like bowers of roses, and a great many of them liked it so much that they turned on every jet in the house, and left them turned on all day, so that in the mere matter of consumption twice as much of my aromatic illuminating air was

"IN THE MATTER OF PERFUME IT WAS FINE"

used in a week as the companies had charged for under the old system, and we used the same metres, too. In addition to this, as a mere life-saving device, my invention proved to have a wonderful value. In the first place nobody could blow it out and be found gas-fixturated the next morning———"

"Good word that—so much more expressive than the old privately owned dictionary word asphyxiated," said the March Hare.

The Hatter nodded his appreciation of the March Hare's compliment, and admitted him once more to his good graces.

"And nobody could commit suicide with it the way they used to do with the old kind of gas, because, you see, it was, after all, only hot air, which is good for the lungs whichever way it's going, in or out. We use hot air

"NOBODY COULD BE GAS-FIXTURATED"

all the time in our Administration and it is wonderful what results you can get from it," he went on. "But it wouldn't light. In fact when anybody tried to light it, such was the pressure, it blew out the match, which I regard as an additional point in its favour. If we have gas that blows out matches the minute the match is applied to it, does not that reduce the chance of fire from the careless habit some people have of throwing lighted matches into the waste-basket?"

"It most certainly does," said the White Knight gravely, and in such tones of finality that Alice did not venture to dispute his assertion.

"We're all agreed upon that point," said the Hatter. "But there were complaints of course. Some people, mostly capitalists who were rich enough to have libraries of their own, complained that they couldn't read nights because the gas wouldn't light. I replied that if they wanted to read they could go to the

Public Library, where there were oil lamps, and electric lights. Besides reading at night is bad for the eyes. Others objected that they couldn't see to go to bed. The answer to that was simple enough. People don't need to see to go to bed. They may need to see when they are dressing in the morning, but when they go to bed all they have to do is to take their clothes off and go, and I added that people who didn't know enough to do that had better have nurses. Finally some of the chief kickers got up a mass-meeting and protested that the new gas wasn't gas at all, and in view of that fact refused to pay their gas tax."

"Oho!" said Alice. "That was pretty serious I should think."

"It seemed so at first," said the Hatter, "but just then the beauty of the Municipal Ownership scheme stepped in. I called a special meeting of the Common Council and they settled the question once for all."

"Good!" cried Alice. "How did they do it?"

"They passed a resolution," said the Hatter, "unanimously declaring the aromatic hot-air to be gas of the most excellent quality, and made it a misdemeanor for anybody to say that it wasn't. I signed the ordinance and from that minute on our gas was gas by law."

"Still," said Alice, "those people had already said it wasn't. Did they back down?"

"Most of 'em did," laughed the Hatter. "And the rest were fined $500 apiece and sent to jail for six months. You see we made the law sufficiently retroactive to grab the whole bunch. Since then there have been no complaints."

Whereupon the Hatter invited Alice to stroll through the gas-plant with him, which the little girl did, and declared it later to have been sweeter than a walk through a rose-garden, which causes me to believe that the Mayor's scheme was a pretty wonderful one after all, and quite worthy of a Hatter thrust by the vagaries of politics into the difficult business of gas making.

CHAPTER IV

THE CITY-OWNED POLICE

AFTER Alice and her companions had enjoyed the aromatic delights of the Blunderland Gas Plant the Hatter and his Cabinet went into executive session for a few hours to decide where they should go next. The interests of Blunderland were so varied that this was a somewhat difficult matter to settle, especially as Mr. Alderman March Hare, who was a great stickler for the rights of the honourable body to which he belonged, wished to have the question referred to a special meeting of the Common Council. The White Knight as Corporation Counsel, however, advised the Hatter that there was no warrant in law compelling him to accede to the March Hare's demand.

"The Municipal Ownership of Rub-
bernecks act has not yet been passed,"
he observed. "Consequently visitors
to our City can be shown about in
any way in which the party in charge
chooses to choose."

"All
right if
you say
so," said
March
Hare
coldly.
"Only I'd
like to
have that
opinion
in writ-
ing. Pub-

"WROTE ON THE SIDE OF A CONVENIENT GAS TANK"

lic officials nowadays are too prune to
deny——"

"Prone, I guess you mean," laughed
the Hatter gleefully.

"I prefer prune," said the March

Hare, with dignity. " Public officials are too prune nowadays to deny what they say in private conversation to encourage me to take any chances."

"Certainly," returned the White Knight. " I'll write it out for you with pleasure." Whereupon, taking a piece of chalk from his pocket, he wrote with it on the side of a convenient gas tank the following opinion:

IN RE WHAT TO DO NEXT

Opinion 7,543,467,223.   *Liber* 29.   *Gas Tank No.* 6

You can go to the People's Shoe Shop,
Or down to the new Town Pump.
You can visit the Civic Glue Shop,
Or call on the Public Chump.

You can visit the Social Rooster,
Or sample Municipal Cheese—
In short you can do what you choose ter,
And go where you dee dash please.

(Signed) JOHN DOE WHITE KNIGHT,
Copperation Counsel.

Meanwhile Alice had been turned over to the Chief of Police to be cared for, and was charmed to discover that that individual was none other than her old friend the Dormouse whom she had met in her trip through Wonderland at the

Hatter's tea-party.

"How did you ever come to be Chief of Police?" she

"I'M THE SOUNDEST SLEEPER IN TOWN"

cried delightedly, as she recognised him.

"I'm the soundest sleeper in town," he replied with a yawn, "so they made me head of the force. You see, young lady, the great trouble with the average police-man is that he's too wide-awake, and that leads to graft. When the Hatter's

Municipal Police Commission looked into
the question they found that the Cop who
spent most of his time asleep spent less of
his time clubbing people who wouldn't
whack up with him on the profits of their
business. Every ossifer who has been
convicted of petty larceny in the past,
the records show, has been a fellow who
stayed awake most of the time, and no
ossifer has ever yet been known to go in
for graft or get a record for clubbing
innocent highwaymen over the head while
he was asleep either on a Park Bench, or
in an alleyway.   Consequently, says they,
Mr. Dormouse who wakes up only on
every fifth Thursday in February will
make the best Police ossifer in the bunch,
and being the best had ought to be chose
chief. Hence accordingly, it became thus.
Moreover I am a champion Tea Drinker."

"What's that got to do with it?"
demanded Alice.

"Everything," said the Dormouse,
rubbing his eyes sleepily. "Every blessed

thing.   Tea Drinking is one of our hardest
duties under the new system providing
for the Municipal Ownership of Everything In Sight Including the Cop on the
Corner.   You see when the City grabbed
up the Bakeries, and the Trolleys, and the
Grand Opera House, and the Condensed
Milk Factory, and the Saw Mills, and the
Breakfast Food Jungles, all envy, hatred
and malice disappeared.   Everybody
loved his neighbour better than he did
himself or his wife's family, and consequently hence there was therefore no
crime, which left the Policeman out of a
job.   The only Burglars left in town were
the regularly appointed official safe-
crackers representing the Municipal Ownership of Petty and Grand Larceny.
The only gambling houses left were under
the direct supervision of the Mayor acting
ex-officio and the Chairman of the Alder-
manic Committee on Faro and Roulette.
The Game of Bunco became a duly
authorised official diversion under con-

trol of the Tax Assessors, and the Town
Toper, being elected by popular vote,
could get as leery as he pleased by public
consent.   Life Insurance Agents became
likewise Public Servants under the General Ordinance of 1905 starting the Civic
Tontine Parlours where people were compelled to buy Life Insurance from the
City itself at so much a yard."

"A yard?" cried Alice.

"Yep," yawned the Dormouse.   "Pol-
icies were issued anywhere from three
inches to a yard long, each inch representing a year.   If you bought a mile of Life
Insurance you were insured for as many
years as there are inches in a mile. I never
could stay awake long enough to figure
out how much that is, but it's several
years."

"But what did the Agents have to
do?" asked Alice.   "If people had to
take it——"

"They went out and grabbed delin-
quents," said the Dormouse.

"I shouldn't think people would need life insurance for the benefit of their families if everybody has everything he wants in Blunderland," put in Alice.

"They don't," said the Dormouse, rapping his head with his club to keep from dropping off to sleep. "It ain't for the benefit of their families—it's for the benefit of the City. A City like this can use benefits to great advantages most all the time. But you see the results of Municipalising all sorts of crime from straight burglary up to life insurance resulted in the Police having nothing to do. There wasn't anybody to arrest, or to quell, or to club, and so they turned us into a social organisation and that's where Tea Drinking comes in strong. Every afternoon at five o'clock, tea is served on every corner in Blunderland by the Policeman on beat. They have become quite a public function, but they're a trifle hard on the police who don't care for tea, because we have to be very polite and take it with everybody who comes up, and be nice and chatty into the bargain. In addition to this we are required to go to dances and take care of the wall-flowers and make ourselves generally agreeable. It is one of

"TEA IS SERVED ON EVERY CORNER"

the laws of Blunderland that all girls are born free and equal in the pursuit of life, liberty and german favours, and when any of the Terpsichorean Force finds a girl with red hair and snub nose with freckles on it decorating the wall and being neglected at a cotillion, it is his duty to plunge in and either dance with her himself, or put some Willieboy under arrest until he calls her out and gives her the time of her life. You can't imagine what wonderful results this Municipal Control of that social situation has done in the line of popularising plain girls."

"It sounds very interesting," Alice ventured. "I should think the girls would like it."

"They do," said the Dormouse. "The only objection to it comes from the Willie-boys, but nobody cares much what they think because there aren't many of them that *can* think."

"And is that all you do?" asked Alice.

"Oh, no indeed," said the Dormouse. "We keep reserves for Bridge Parties at the Station all the time, so that if any taxpayer ever needs a fourth hand to make up a game all he has to do is to ring up headquarters and get an ossifer to come up and play. In addition to this we look after old ladies who want to go shopping and aren't strong enough to break through the rush line at the bargain counters. And then once in a while somebody's baby will wake up at three o'clock in the morning and demand the moon, and we go up and attend to it."

"What?" cried Alice in amazement. "You don't mean to say you give it the moon?"

"Not exactly," said the Dormouse. "We just promise to give it. That's one of the strong points about Municipal Ownership. It's the easiest system to make promises under you ever knew. You can promise anything, and later on if you don't make good you can promise something better, and so on. It works very well in a great many places.

"But that isn't really what we go up to the house for. We go up to relieve the poor tired parents who have been working hard all day and are too weary to walk up and down the floor with the baby. We respond immediately to the call, grab up the baby and walk the floor with him until he is quiet again. Once last winter a chap with three pairs of twins six months, a year and a half, and three years old respectively, had to send for the patrol wagon. All six of 'em

"WE RESPOND IMMEDIATELY TO THE CALL"

waked up and began to squall at once and we sent seven ossifers and a sergeant up to look after them. They had to parade around that house from 2 A. M. until seven-thirty before those babies quit yelling."

Just at this moment the Dormouse

was interrupted in his story by a raggedly dressed old man on a pair of crutches who begged an alms of him.

"Only a dollar, sir," he asked piteously. "Only a dollar to relieve a terrible case of distress."

"Certainly, Simpkins," said the Dormouse kindly. "I—well I'll be jiggered—" he added, feeling through his pockets. "I must have left my money at home. Maybe this young lady can help you out. Miss Alice, permit me to introduce you to Simpkins. He's the most successful beggar in nineteen counties."

"Glad to meet you," said Alice, shaking hands with Simpkins.

"You couldn't spare a dollar, could you, Miss?" whined the Beggar. "It will relieve a terrible case of distress Ma'am."

"Why—yes," said Alice, suddenly remembering that she had a silver dollar in her pocket. "Here it is."

And she handed it to Simpkins who thanked her profusely.

"How's business?" asked the Dormouse.

"Fine," said Simpkins, executing a

jig.   "I've collected $800 since eleven o'clock this morning."

Whereupon, f o r g e t-ting his crutches, he made off up the street with the

"MADE OFF WITH THE AGILITY OF AN ANTELOPE"

agility of an antelope.   Alice gazed after him in wonder.

"I—I didn't suppose you had any beggars in Blunderland," said she.

"He's the only one," replied the Dormouse.   "He's the official Beggar of the

Town.   He gets $25,000 in Tenth De-
ferred Reorganisation Certificates a year
—which, if the Certificates pay ten cents
on the dollar, as we hope, will turn out to
be a good salary in the end."

"But why does he beg? Who gets the
money?" asked Alice.

"The City," said the Dormouse. "Once
in a while when the Printing Plant gets
clogged up with large orders of Bonds for
our various enterprises, the City has to
get hold of a few dollars of real money, so
they send Simpkins out for it.   I believe
he's out to-day trying to raise the interest on the Sixteenth Mortgage Extension
Bonds on the Municipal Cigarette Plant
purchased year before last.   It's ten
months overdue and the former owners
have asked the Government to smoke
up."

"Oh!" said Alice.   "Is the Printing
Plant clogged up?"

"Unmercifully," said the Dormouse.
"Not to say teetotally.   They're prepar-

ing their Christmas issues in Magazine form, and that means a terrible lot of extra work. I don't believe the way things look now that the City will be able to print the money for last January's pay-roll until somewhere around the next Fourth of July, and if that's the case poor old Simpkins will either have to work overtime or get a half-dozen Deputy Assistant Beggars to put the town in funds. I'm expecting to have the Police put on that job at any minute."

Alice was silent for a moment, and the Dormouse went on.

"What do you think of the Municipal Ownership of the Police idea?" he asked.

"It's fine," said Alice. "But I thought all Cities owned their police force."

"A great many people think that," laughed the Dormouse. "But it isn't so."

"It is in New York and Chicago—I heard my Papa say so once," said Alice.

Again the Dormouse laughed.

"Well," he said. "I don't want to cast any asparagus on your father's intelligence, but he's wrong. The Police may own New York and Chicago, but New York and Chicago don't own the police—not by a long shot."

"Who does, then?" demanded Alice.

"The Lord only knows," laughed the Dormouse. "Some people say John Doe, and other people say the Man Higher Up, but which it is, or who either of 'em may be, I haven't the slightest idea. Maybe they belong to the Copper Trust."

And then with a sly wink at the little maid the Dormouse turned over and went to sleep.

CHAPTER V

THE MUNICIPAPHONE

ARMED with the Copperation Counsel's opinion authorising him to do whatever he pleased next, the Hatter decided that he would give Alice a

"YOU CAN TALK ALL YOU PLEASE"

demonstration of the workings of the Municipaphone.

"Which," said he proudly, "I consider to be the most Democraticising thing I have ever invented. You can talk all you please about Universal Brotherhood, Unlimited Sisterhood, and the Infinity of Unclehood, but all of these movements put together haven't done as much to promote the equality of everybody as that Municipaphone idea of mine."

Alice thought the Cheshire Cat's grin expanded slightly as the Hatter spoke, but she was not sure, although he most assuredly did wink at her.

"I should admire to see it," she said. "What is it, just?"

"It is the result of the Municipal Ownership of the Telephone," returned the Hatter proudly. "We have taken over everything that works by electricity —electric lighting, the telegraph, the telephone——"

"Even the thunder and lightning," interrupted the White Knight. "And under our management everything runs so smoothly that even the lightning doesn't strike any more. That's a great thing in Municipal Ownership. There aren't any more strikes under it."

"What he says is true, my child," said the Hatter, "and in time we expect to get the thunder itself under control so that it will serve some useful purpose—I don't know yet exactly what, but I am having experiments made in storage batteries which will catch and hold the thunder with the idea of saving the noise it makes for fire-crackers, or Presidential salutes, or other things and occasions where the fracturing of silence seems desirable. Surely if we can take electricity and under suitable Municipal supervision make it serve as a substitute for a tallow dip, why shouldn't we extract the reverberance with which it is fraught to add to the general clangour of joyous occasions?"

"No reason at all," said Alice. "I wonder no one has ever thought of that before.   Just think of all the magnificent noises that go to waste in a thunder-storm.''

"You will discover in time, my dear child, that only under the Municipal Ownership of Brains such as we have here, can such great ideas be seized from the infinity of nothingness and turned into an irresistible propaganda,'' said the Hatter loftily.

"He's the biggest gander of the bunch,'' whispered the March Hare.

"But it isn't what we are going to do, but what we have done that we propose to show you,'' continued the Hatter, eyeing the March Hare coldly.   "And as I have said, the Municipaphone is my crowning achievement.   Just come here and I will show you.''

The Hatter led Alice to a nearby lamp-post, and pointing to a little box fastened to the middle of the pillar explained to her that that was the Municipaphone.

"We have them in every room in

every house in the City, on all the lamp-posts, hydrants, telegraph poles, in fact everywhere where there is a chance or room enough to hang one," the Hatter explained.

"It's just like a telephone, isn't it?" said Alice. "Only it looks like a hat instead of a funnel."

"Exactly," said the Hatter, "but we don't call it a telephone any more. The word telephone struck me as being a misnomer. You don't tell the 'phone anything when you talk into it. You tell the person at the other end of the line, and so, I changed its name to the Municipaphone, which shows that it's a 'phone that belongs to the City. Just to sort of moralise the thing I had the mouth-piece changed to look like a hat instead of a funnel, because funnels are apt to suggest alcoholic beverages and sometimes people who aren't at all thirsty are made so by the mere power of suggestion. The hat, however, has always commended itself to our greatest statesmen as a vehicle best suited for the transmission of ideas, and I therefore adopted it.''

"It is very pretty," commented Alice. "Only I think a few ribbons would improve it a little.''

"Possibly," said the Hatter. "We haven't had time yet to look after the millinery aspect of the situation, but we'll take that up at our next Cabinet meeting. I thank you for the suggestion. But you see how the thing works. This little book here has a list of the names of everybody in town with their Municipa-phone numbers attached. The lowly as well as the highly, from the newsboy up to the Bridge Whist set, are all repre-sented here, so that all are connected in one way or another with each other. There is no man, woman, or child so poor and humble of birth, that he or she cannot get into immediate relations with the haughty and proud. Everybody is on speaking terms with everybody else, and we have thereby reached socially a condition wherein all men though not related are nevertheless connected. You frequently hear a wash-lady remark that while she has not met Mrs. Van Varick Van Astorbilt or Mrs. Willieboy de Crudoil personally, they are nevertheless connections of hers if not by blood or marriage at least by wire, which is stronger than either. Some day instead of having Societies of the Cincinnati, and Sons and Daughters of the Revolution I hope to see associations of Brothers and Sisters of the Municipaphone which shall become a factor of overwhelming solidarity in all social and political affairs."

"It's a splendid scheme," said Alice.

"It is a tie of material strength which binds together our first and last families, increasing the pride of the latter, and diminishing that of the former until we have at last reached an average of self-satisfaction which knows no barriers of class distinction," said the Hatter. "But it wouldn't have worked if we hadn't formulated strict rules by which every household in town is governed. One of our rules is that the person called upon must answer immediately and truthfully any question which the person at the other end asks, and of course in perfectly polite language. For instance, suppose you try it yourself. Just ring up Number 83115, Bloomingdale, and ask for Mrs. S. Van Livingston Smythe. She's the biggest swell in town. Ask her anything that comes into your head, and you'll see how it works. Tell her you are Mrs. O'Flaherty, the Head Wash-Lady of the Municipal Laundry."

Alice took her place at the Municipa-phone and called 83115 Bloomingdale, as instructed.

"Hello!" she said.

"Hush! Don't say that—say Ah there!" interrupted the Hatter. "Hello comes under the head of profanity, which is against the law."

"Excuse me," said Alice. "Ah there!" she added. "Give me 83115 Bloomingdale, please, Central."

"Name, please," said Central.

"Bridget O'Flaherty," replied Alice

"Address?" asked Central.

"Tub 37, Municipal Laundry," said Alice.

"Occupation?" continued the other.

"Wringer," laughed Alice.

"All right, there you are," said Central, making the desired connection.

"Is this Mrs. S. Van Livingston Smythe?" asked Alice.

"Yes," said a sweet voice from the other end of the line. "What is it?"

"I am Bridget O'Flaherty," said Alice, "of the Municipal Laundry, and I wanted to ask was your grandfather ever a monkey?"

It was not a very polite question, but under the excitement of the moment Alice could think of nothing better to ask.

"I don't believe so, Mrs. O'Flaherty," came the sweet voice in answer. "I have looked over every branch of our family tree and there isn't a cocoanut on it. Why, are you looking for a missing grandfather of your own?"

"No," smiled Alice, "but I've read all the books in the public library and I thought he might have a tail to tell that I would find amusing."

"Well, I'm very sorry," said the sweet voice. "Grandfather died forty years ago, so I don't believe he can help you. I would advise you to go up to the Monkeyhouse and ask one of your own brothers. Good-bye."

"Good-bye," said Alice.

"Well?" asked the Hatter with a grin. "What do you think of it?"

"Why—it's perfectly wonderful," said Alice. "If that were to happen in New York or even in Brooklyn or Binghamton Mrs. S. Van Livingston Smythe would have been very indignant, not only over the question, but for the mere fact that the—er—wash-lady dared ring her up at all."

"Exactly," said the Hatter, with a bland smile of satisfaction. "This Municipaphone controlled by strict rules which people must obey is a great social leveller."

"But why did Central want my name and address?" asked Alice.

"Because Central has to keep a record of all that everybody says for the Inspector of Personal Communications," explained the Hatter. "Every word you and Mrs. Smythe spoke was recorded at the Central Office, and if either of you had used any expression stronger than Fudge, or O Tutt you would have been fined five dollars for each expression and repetition thereof. We expect to establish Civic Control of Public and Private Speech within the next year, and we have begun it with supervision of the Municipaphone."

"But, cried Alice, "If I had said

something that required a fine, wouldn't Mrs. O'Flaherty, who is innocent, have had to pay?"

"Yes," said the Hatter. "But in all cases where the public welfare is con-

"FINED FIVE DOLLARS"

cerned, private interests must yield however great the hardship. That is one of the fundamental principles of Municipal Ownership. Mrs. O'Flaherty would have to suffer in order that the great principle involved in Polite Speech for all Classes might prevail. The strict enforcement of our anti-Gosh legislation has resulted almost in the complete elimination of profane speech in Blunderland—so much so in fact that in the new Dictionary we are compiling such words as Golramit, Dodgastit, and Goshallhemlocks are being left out altogether."

"It is a great moral agency," said the White Knight. "It increases the self-respect of the submerged, curbs the pride of the rich, and holds in complete subjection those evil communications which corrupt good manners."

"And nothing but the result of Municipal Owner- ship," put in the March Hare enthusi- astically, for- getting his grouch for a moment.

"It has other advan- tages, too," said the Hatter, "to which I

"THE DICTIONARY WE ARE COMPILING"

"ALICE TRANSFIXED AT THE PHONE"

feel I should call your attention. These phones being in every room in town with which anybody may be connected at any moment and thus overhear what other people are saying, gossip is gradually dying out, and people everywhere are more careful of what they say even in private, for nowadays the walls literally have ears. To give you an example, I will connect you at once with the home of the Duchess whom you met, if you remember, in your journey through Wonderland and you may judge for yourself of how useful this Municipaphone is to us in ascertaining the general trend of public opinion."

The Hatter gave the order to Central and in a minute Alice stood transfixed at the phone listening intently.   She recognised the voice of the Duchess immediately.

"THE BIGGEST JACKASS FROM DAN TO BEERSHEBA"

"As for that old fool of a Hatter," she was saying, "he is the biggest jackass from Dan to Beersheba."

"Well?" said the Hatter.   "Can you hear her?"

"Yes," giggled Alice. "Very plainly."

"What does she say?" asked the Hatter, simpering.

"Why," said Alice reddening, "she—she's talking about you."

"The dear Duchess," ejaculated the Hatter, with a foolish smirk. "I'm very much afraid—ahem—that the Duchess has her eye on me."

"She has," said Alice. "She is referring to you in the warmest tones—she thinks you're big—great—the very greatest from Dan to Beersheba."

"Ah me!" sighed the Hatter. "If I were only a younger man!"

"They'll make a match of it yet," said the White Knight in a soft whisper to Alice.

"Yes," sneered the March Hare, who had overheard, jealously, "and a fine old sulphur-headed lucifer of a match it will be too."

"Well, it's all very nice," said Alice, very anxious to change the subject. "But I can't say that I'm sure I'd like it. Why, you can't have any secrets from anybody."

"And why should you wish to, my dear child?" asked the Hatter, coming out of his dream of romance. "Why not so order your life that you have no need for secrecy?"

"Yes," said Alice. "I suppose that is better, but then, Mr. Hatter, isn't there to be any more private life?"

"Not under Municipal Ownership," said the Hatter. "Carried to its logical conclusion that with all other so-called private rights will be merged in the glorious culmination of a complete well rounded Municipal Life. It is toward that Grand Civic Eventuation that I and my associates in this noble movement are constantly striving."

"Are you going to have Municipal Control of Marriage?" asked Alice, slyly.

The Hatter blushed and smiled foolishly. "I ah—am thinking about that," he said with a funny little laugh. "It would be a most excellent thing to do, for in my opinion a great many people nowadays

get married too thoughtlessly. Just because they happen to love each other
they go off and get married, but under
Municipal Control it would be much
more difficult for a man or a woman to
take so serious a step. For instance,
if I had my way the Common Council
would have to be asked for permission
for a man to marry. The question would
come up in the form of a bill, which would
immediately be referred to the Committee
on Matrimony, who would discuss it very
thoroughly before bringing it before the
Council. If a majority of the Committee
considered that the application should
be granted, then the matter should be
placed before the whole Council, by which
it should be debated in open public ses-
sions, the applicant having been invited
to appear and under cross-examination
by the District Attorney demonstrate
his fitness to be married. All others
knowing any reason why he should not
be married should also have the oppor-

tunity to appear and state their reasons for opposing the granting of the application. I am inclined to believe that this would put a stop to these hasty marriages which have given rise to that beautiful proverb, Married in Camden, Repent at South Dakota."

"I should think it would," said Alice. "And when do you propose to start this plan along?"

"Well, you see," said the Hatter with a giggle, "before I take final steps in the matter I wish to have a few words with—er—well—you know who—I——"

"The Duchess," Alice ventured.

"Ah, you precocious child!" cried the Hatter, tapping Alice on the shoulder coyly. "You must not believe all you overhear the Duchess say about me. She is so prejudiced, and blind to my faults. I—I'm almost sorry I connected you with her over the Municipaphone."

CHAPTER VI

THE DEPARTMENT OF PUBLIC VERSE

I THINK," said the Hatter, "that before we go any further we would better show Miss Alice our Municipal Poetry Factory. The whistle will blow very shortly and our Divine Afflatus Dynamo will shut down, so if she is to see that feature of our work now is the time to do it."

"Yes," said the March Hare, "although the office is in some confusion owing to your recent Municipal Order Number 20,367 making *Alabazam* rhyme with *Mulligatawney*, and extending the number of lines in the municipal quatrains from four to twenty-three. The employees are finding considerable difficulty in making twenty-three-line quatrains and at least half the force have gone home suffering from acute attacks of brainstormitis."

"It'll do 'em good," laughed the Hatter. "A good brain storm may result in a few of them being struck. Come along, Miss Alice, and we'll show you our City Poets at work."

"I don't think I understand," said Alice. "What is a city poet?"

"He bears the same relation to Municipal Poetry that a White Wing bears to the Street Cleaning Department," explained the Hatter. "Two years ago the City took over all the Verse-making enterprises of Blunderland, appointed a Municipalaureat, otherwise a Commissioner of Public Verse, and started him along with a Department. He employs 16,743 poets who provide all the poetry that is consumed by our people. It has resulted in great good for everybody. Poetry is cheaper by eight cents a line than it used to be, and, as you may have guessed from what the March Hare has just said, we give larger measure than was the custom under the private owner-ship of *Pegasus*. Quatrains have been increased from four lines to twenty-three, and the old stingy fourteen-line sonnet has been enlarged to fifty-four lines. We

"LARGER MEASURE THAN WAS
THE CUSTOM"

have also passed an ordinance requiring that poems shall say what they mean, which is a vast im-provement on the old private control meth-od whereunder any-body was allowed to write rhymes which nobody could under-stand—like that thing of Miss Arethusa Spink's, for instance, called Aspiration. Remember that?"

"I don't think I ever heard it," said Alice.

"Well it went this way," said the

Hatter, and striking a graceful attitude he recited the following lines called:

ASPIRATION

By Arethusa Spink

Down by the purple opalescent sea,
  Flung like a ribbon limp athwart the sky,
A rose lay blooming on the restless lea,
While sundry birds came chattering sweetly by.
'Twas then my soul that all too long had slept,
  Awoke from out its iridescent nap,

[crept
Down where the pink-cheeked crocus blossoms
  From out fair Nature's over-bounteous lap,
And cried aloud "Alas! What hath betode?
  What dream is this that like the ambient brook
Forbids the mind to face the solemn goad
    And know itself forsook!

The Hatter paused.

"Well?" said Alice, slightly puzzled.

"That's all there was to it," said the Hatter. "It was printed in one of our Magazines and within forty-eight hours the ambulance from the Insane Asylum

was called out 737 times by people who
had gone crazy trying to find out what
it meant. It capped the climax. I
called a special meeting of the Common
Council to take the matter up purely as
a matter of public health, and before I
went to bed that night they had passed
and I had signed an Act giving the control of the Verse Industry to the City
and taking it out of the hands of irre-
sponsible, unlicensed independent poets."

"And a good job it was too," said
the March Hare.

"And you chose one of the best poets
in town for the Commissioner, I suppose?"
suggested Alice.

"No we didn't," said the Hatter.   "I
didn't want any Moonshine in a City
Department and no poet is a good business man. I picked out a very successful Haberdasher in the Sixth Ward
for the delicate business of organising the
Department, and he has done most excellent work.   We found that just as a first

class confectioner made a splendid mana-
ger of our Gas plant, and a successful
Hoki-Poki merchant had the required
push to keep our trolley systems going,
so the Haberdasher had the precise kind
of genius to manage the poets. He won't
stand any nonsense from them, and any
poem that he can't understand is immediately thrown into the Civic Waste-
Basket, taken to the Municipal Ferry
and used for fuel to run the boats. I
guess we burn nineteen tons of refuse
verse a day, don't we, Alderman?"

"About that—on the average, "said
the March Hare. "Sometimes it gets
as high as twenty tons and occasionally
it falls off to sixteen—but using these
rejected manuscripts in place of coal has
reduced the loss on the Ferry about
thirty-eight dollars a year in real money."

"How much is that in bonds?" asked
Alice slyly.

"O—let's see," said the Hatter, his
face getting very red, "well—I should

say on a basis of $43\frac{1}{3}\%$ to one, thirty-eight dollars would come to about $97,347.83 in third debenture ten per cent. certificates, exclusive of the cost of printing, advertising, and the number we give away as sample copies."

"Quite a saving," said Alice.

"Yes," said the Hatter. "We save all we can. Economy in real money is our watchword. We never spend a cent where a bond will serve the purpose."

By this time Alice and her hosts had reached the building occupied by the Department of Public Verse, and upon entering its spacious doorway the party were greeted by the Commissioner, the Haberdasher, to whom Alice was promptly introduced. He reminded her very forcibly of her old acquaintance Bill the Lizard, but she was not sure enough on this point to recall their previous meeting when she had so tactlessly kicked him up through the chimney flue of the Wonderland Cottage.

"Well, Mr. Commissioner," said the Hatter, "how are you getting along?"

"Pretty well, Mr. Mayor," replied the Commissioner. "We've just finished the

"GREETED BY THE COMMISSIONER, THE HABERDASHER"

six line couplet for the new Chewing Gum Bonds."

"Good," said the Hatter. "How does it go?"

"Rather neatly I think," said the Commissioner, and he read the following:

> We promise to pay
> This bond some day
> If of the stuff
> We've got enough.
> And if we haven't, pray don't despond,
> For we'll pay it off with another bond.

"Fine," said the Hatter. "You strike a very lofty note in that. And how do the new Limericks work?"

"We've finished number 3907 of series XZV," said the Commissioner. "I'll send for Wiggins who wrote it and let him read it to you himself."

"IT RUNS THIS WAY, YOUR HONOUR"

A pressure of an electric button brought the smiling Wiggins into the office.

"Wiggins, the Mayor would like

to hear that new Limerick of yours,"
said the Commissioner.

"Thanky sir," said Wiggins. "It
runs this way, your honour.

> There was an old lady named Jane
> Who sat on a fence at Schoharie.
> A rooster came by
> And crew like the deuce
> But Jane never scared for a cent.

"That's great," said the Hatter.
"Don't you think so, Miss Alice?"

"Why yes," said Alice, "but—does it
rhyme?"

"Perfectly," replied the Hatter, "that
is, under our system. When we organ-
ised this Department to facilitate business and avoid the waste of time looking
for rhymes we legalised such rhymes as
Schoharie and cent and by and deuce.
By that act we found that where one man
could only turn out 800 Limericks a day
under the old system, any ablebodied-
poet can write 3,000 in the same number

of hours. That's very good, Wiggins," he added turning to the workman. "I shall recommend the Commissioner to promote you to an Inspectorship in the Sonnet works."

"Thanky sir," said the Poet, as he blushingly bowed himself out.

"OUR THINKING DEPARTMENT"

"Here," said the Commissioner, opening a door leading into a long, darkened chamber, "here, young lady, is our Thinking Department."

Alice passed into the darkness and dimly made out a half a hundred long-haired individuals sitting in comfortable Morris chairs, their forefingers pressed hard against their brows and their eyes gazing fixedly out into space.

"These men and women think the thoughts which our municipal poetry is designed to express," the Commissioner continued. "A thought once seized by any one of them is written down upon a pad, and then taken into this next room where it is classified and assigned to the line cutters who turn out the first draft in the rough. Then when this is done it is sent to the rhyming room where the lines are made to end in rhymes, and finally it goes to the Polishing room where the poem is made ready for publication."

"It's a wonderful system," said the Hatter. "It not only improves the quality of our poetry, but in campaign times it is a great help, since we control absolutely all the campaign poetry. When I run for mayor next fall to succeed myself there won't be a single poem written on the other side."

"That ought to be a great help," said Alice.

"Yes," said the Hatter. "It will be. Every employee in this Department will not only vote for me but will work for me as well. Same way in the gas plant and the trolley—in fact in all the City Departments. It is only another evidence of the very great value of Municipal Ownership. It is uncertainty in political times that upsets business, but with the Municipality in control of all these Departments from Gas to Poetry there is no uncertainty about who will win, so that business is not unsettled by it."

"Wonderful," said Alice.

"By the way, Mr. Commissioner, you'd better start the Rhyming Bureau on the search for rhymes to Hatter at once," said the Mayor. "We don't want to be caught unprepared at the last minute."

"The list is being compiled now," replied the Commissioner. "We already have, Matter, Batter, Tatter, Smatter Patter, Ratter, Spatter and Scatter."

"Fine!" chortled the Hatter.

"Don't forget Chatter," put in Alice.

"Thank you—I'll make a note of it," said the Commissioner.

"And Snatter," growled the March Hare gloomily, who evidently felt that somebody ought to be looking for rhymes to March Hare as well.

"What does snatter mean?" demanded the Hatter frowning.

"It's a corrupt form for snatcher," retorted the March Hare. "One who snatches everything he can lay his hands on, without regard to whether it's his by divine right or not. I guess they can use it in poems calling attention to your Civic Virtues."

"Except by unanimous vote of the Common Council over my veto Snatter stays out of the Municipal Vocabulary," returned the Hatter coldly. "Your own confession that it is corrupt is enough to condemn it with me."

"I wouldn't use batter either, Mr. Mayor," said the Commissioner. "Batter is dough and we haven't got any worth mentioning."

"It is also to whack, slam, bang,

bust, smack," retorted the Hatter, "so your recommendation is not accepted. Seems to me I can almost hear the campaign clubs singing as they march:

O the noble, noble Hatter,
Ain't he grand!
How his enemies do scatter
Thro the land!
How his foemen he doth batter
With their idle gloomy chatter
On this Muni—cipal Matter
Beats the band!

"O Gee!" ejaculated the March Hare. "Do you call that poetry?"

"Sir, I call it truth," returned the Hatter, "and poetry is truth just as art is truth, and if you don't believe it all you've got to do is to try and run against me next fall on that issue. I'll beat you to a stand-still."

"Of course you will," sighed the March Hare. "But you wouldn't but for that last ordinance you jammed through while I was off on my vacation."

"What was that?" demanded the Hatter.

"Giving the Election Commission absolute control over the votes, and then appointing yourself Election Commissioner ex-officio," said the March Hare. "I don't believe that Municipal Control of the ballot is constitutional."

"Well, it will be constitutional," said the Hatter drily.

"When?" demanded the March Hare.

"When we secure Municipal Control of the Constitution," said the Hatter. "I'll make it Constitutional if I have to rewrite the whole blessed Constitution myself."

Whereupon the Hatter walked majestically forth into the street once more, and Alice and the March Hare together with the White Knight followed meekly in his train.

CHAPTER VII

OWNERSHIP OF CHILDREN

WHAT time is it?" asked the Hatter, suddenly turning to the White Knight.

"Six o'clock," replied the White Knight, looking at his watch.

"Mercy!" cried Alice. "I had no idea it was so late! I shall have to run along home—it's supper time."

The Hatter laughed.

"O, as for that," he said, "there's no hurry. Under our present system of Municipal Ownership of Everything, I can issue, as Mayor, a general order postponing the Municipal Supper Hour to seven or eight o'clock. Still—if you'd prefer to go home——"

"I don't want to," said Alice courteously, "but I think I'd better. My mother would be worried not finding me in the nursery. You see, I left home without telling anybody where I was going."

Again the Hatter laughed.

"What foolishness!" he ejaculated. "That's the great trouble with the private ownership of children. It worries their poor mothers, keeps 'em from their daily Bridge parties, interferes with that freedom of action which is guaranteed to the individual by the contravention of the United States——"

"Constitution, I guess you mean," suggested Alice.

"It used to be the Constitution," returned the Hatter, " but now it's the Contravention. It has been contravened so often in the past few years that our Reformed Language Commission at Washington has named it accordingly."

"It simply bears out what you said in your message approving the Public Ownership of Children Act passed by the Common Council last November, which I wrote for you, and consequently consider a very able document," said the White Knight.

"The Public Ownership of Children?" cried Alice, with a look of alarm on her face.

"Yes," said the Hatter. "Just as the Nation has gone in for paternalism, we here in Blunderland have gone in for maternalism. The children here belong to the city——"

"But——" Alice began.

"Now, don't bother," said the Hatter kindly. "It works very well. It has reduced children to a state of scientific control which is as careful and as effective as that of the street cleaning department or the public parks, and it has emancipated the mothers as well as materially decreased the financial obligations of the fathers."

Alice's lip quivered slightly, and she began to feel a little bit afraid of the Hatter.

"I want to go home," she whimpered.

"Certainly—as you wish," said the Hatter. "We'll take you there at once. Come along."

Reassured by the Hatter's kindly manner Alice took her companion's outstretched hand and they walked along the highway together until they came to a handsome apartment house fronting upon a beautiful park, where the Hatter pressed an electric button at one side of the massive entrance. The response to the bell was immediate, and Alice was pleased to find that the person to answer was none other than the Duchess herself.

"Why, how-di-doo," said the Duchess affably. "Glad to see you again, Miss Alice."

"Thank you," said Alice. "It is very nice to be here. Do you live in this beautiful building?"

"Yes," said the Duchess. "You see, I've just been appointed Commissioner of Maternity. I'm what you might call the official mother of the town. Since that great Statesman, the Hatter"—here the Duchess winked graciously at the March Hare—"devised his crowning achievement in the Municipal Control of the Children and appointed me to be the Head of the Department, I have been stationed here."

"And a mighty good old mother she is!" ejaculated the Hatter with fervour.

"Palaverer!" said the Duchess coyly.

"Not at all," said the Hatter. "I speak not as a man, but as a Mayor, and what I say is to be construed as an official tribute to a faithful and deserving public servant."

"Servant, sir?" repeated the Duchess haughtily.

"In the American sense," said the Hatter with a low bow. "In the sense that the servant is as good as, if not better than the employer, Madam."

"That man's a perfect Dipsomaniac," said the March Hare.

"Diplomat, man—diplomat," corrected the White Knight. "A dipsomaniac is a very different thing from a Diplomat. Consuls may be dipsomaniacs, but a Diplomat is a man worthy of Ambassadorial honours."

"Oh—I see," said the March Hare. "Well—he's a Diplomat all right, all right."

"How are things going to-day, Duchess?" asked the Hatter. "Children happy?"

"They will be in time," said the Duchess. "So many of them have been brought up so far on the *Ladies' Home Journal* system that it is hard to introduce the new Blunderland method without friction."

"I was afraid of that," said the Hatter. "How does the compulsory soda-water regulation work?"

"Splendidly," said the Duchess.

"Since I started in in January to make the children drink five glasses of Vanilla Cream soda every day as a matter of routine and duty, sixty per cent. of them have come to hate it. I think that by the end of the year we shall have stamped out the love of soda almost entirely. The same way with caramels and other candies in place of beef. We have caramels for breakfast, gum-drops for dinner and marshmallows for tea, regularly, and last night seventeen of the children presented a petition asking for beefsteak, mutton chops and boiled rice. I have a firm conviction that when the new law, requiring beef to be sold at candy stores, and compelling those in charge of the young to teach them that boiled rice and hominy are bad for the teeth, goes into effect, we shall find the children clamouring for wholesome food as eagerly as they do now for things that ruin their little tummies."

"It's a splendid system—and how

are you meeting the matinee problem?" asked the March Hare.

"Same way," said the Duchess. "Every Wednesday and Saturday afternoon we make 'em go to a matinee, rain or shine, whether they want to or not, and really it's pathetic to see how some of the little dears pine for a half-holiday with a hoople, and since I forbade the youngsters to even look at the back of a geography, or a spelling book, it is most amusing to see how they sneak into the library and devour the contents of those two books when they think nobody's looking. I caught one of the boys reading an Arithmetic in bed last night, wholly neglecting his Jack Harkaway books that I had commanded him to read, and leaving his 'Bim, the Broncho Buster of Buffalo,' absolutely uncut."

"Fine!" chuckled the Hatter. "And now, my dear Duchess, will you oblige me by taking charge of Miss Alice? She has expressed a desire to go home and so I have brought her here."

"Certainly," said the Duchess. "I'll look after her."

"You'll excuse us, Alice," said the

"WHEN THEY THINK NOBODY'S LOOKING"

Hatter, politely. "We'd escort you further ourselves, but a question has come before the Municipal Ownership Caucus that we must settle before the meeting of the Common Council to-night. Certain of our members claim that they have a right to sell their votes for $500 apiece——"

"Mercy!" cried Alice. "Why, that is—that is terrible."

"It certainly is," said the March Hare ruefully. "It's more than terrible, it's rotten. Here I've been holding out for $1,250 for mine, and these duffers want to go in for a cut rate that will absolutely ruin the business."

"It's a very important matter," said the Hatter. "After all our striving to elevate the people we don't want them to make themselves too cheap. For my part I don't think they should let go of a vote on any question for less than $2,500."

"That's all right, Mr. Mayor," said the White Knight. "But you don't want to frighten capital, you know."

"Well, you and I disagree on that point," said the Mayor. "Capital isn't at all necessary to the success of our schemes. My watchword is Bonds, and as long as I have a printing press to print 'em, and a fountain pen to sign 'em I'm not going to be influenced one way or another by a feeling of subserviency to the capitalist class. Good night, Miss Alice. Glad to have met you and I hope you will have a pleasant time with the Duchess. Here," he added, taking a beautifully printed green and gold paper from his pocket, "here is a Blanket Mortgage 18% Deferred Debenture Bond on the Main Street Ferry of a par value of $100,000 payable in 3457, as a souvenir of your visit."

"A hundred thousand dollars," cried Alice. "For me?"

"No," corrected the Hatter. "A hundred thousand dollar bond. You don't get the money until 3457, and not then unless you present it in person to the City Treasurer."

With which munificent gift the Hatter respectfully bowed himself away and made off, followed by the March Hare.

"Good-bye, Alice," said the White

Knight sympathetically; and then thrusting a paper in her hand, he leaned forward and whispered into the little girl's ear, "If you get into trouble, use this."

"Thank you," said Alice. "What is it?"

"It's a temporary injunction issued by the Chief Justice restraining anybody from interfering with you," said the White Knight. "You may need it."

And the kindly old knight ran madly off up the

"IF YOU GET INTO TROUBLE, USE THIS"

street after the Mayor and the March Hare, and shortly after disappeared around the corner.

"Now, my little dear," said the Duchess, "we'll take you home."

Seizing Alice by the hand the Duchess led the little traveller into the Municipal Nursery. Entering the elevator, they went up and up and up and up until Alice thought they would never stop. Finally on the 117th floor the elevator stopped. Alice and the Duchess alighted and entered a funny little flat, singularly enough labelled with Alice's own name.

"This is it," said the Duchess. "There is your bedroom, here is your parlour, and that is the bath-room. The apartment has running soda-water, hot and cold; you will find a refrigerator stocked with peanut brittle, molasses candy, and sugared fruits in the pantry. Your reading will consist of Lucy the Lace Vendor, or How the Laundress Became a Lady; the works of Marie Corelli; Factory Fanny, the Forger's Daughter, and any other unwholesome book you may want from the House of Correction Library. Playtime will begin at seven every morning and you will be compelled to dress and undress dolls until one, when your caramel will be given to you, after which you will skip the rope and read fairy stories until six. You must drink five glasses of soda-water every day and will not be allowed to go to bed before eleven o'clock at night. Hurry now, and get your hair mussed and your hands dirty for dinner. The first course of whipped cream and roasted chestnuts will be served promptly at six-thirty."

"But," cried Alice, "I don't want to stay here—I want to go home."

"You are home," said the Duchess. "This is the Municipal Home of the Children of Blunderland."

"But I want my father and mother," whimpered Alice.

"The City is your father, my child, and I am officially your mother," said the Duchess.

"You are not!" cried Alice. "You are trying to kidnap me!—I'll—I'll call the police."

"The police can't arrest a city, my dear child, and as for me as the Commissioner of Maternity I am immune from arrest," laughed the Duchess.

"Well, I just won't stay, that's all," cried Alice, stamping her foot angrily. "I don't want a city for a father, and I shan't have an official mother in place of a real one."

"SEIZING HER BY THE ARM"

The child ran toward the door, but the Duchess was too quick for her, seizing her by the arm.

"Let me go!" shrieked Alice.

"Never," snapped the Duchess.

And then the little girl thought of the piece of paper the White Knight had given her.

"I guess that will make you change your mind," she said, handing the injunction to her captor.

The Duchess read it carefully; her face paled, and she too stamped her foot.

"I'll see about this," she roared angrily, and in a moment she had gone, slamming the door so hard behind her that the building fairly shook. A moment later Alice followed, and in a short time was bounding down the stairway as fast as her little legs would carry her toward freedom, when all of a sudden she tripped and began to fall—down, down, down—O, would she never stop! And then, bump! Her fall was over, and strange to relate the little maid found herself sitting on the floor back in her own nursery in her own real home, with her mother bending over her.

"Dear me, Alice," said her mother. "I hope you haven't hurt yourself."

"No," said Alice. "Why—have I —I really fallen?"

"You most certainly have—off the sofa," laughed her mother. "Where

"WHY—HAVE I—I REALLY FALLEN?"

have you been?" she added. "In Wonderland again?"

"No," said Alice. "In Blunderland —this time."

Which struck her father, when he heard the story of her adventures later, as a very apt and descriptive title for the M. O. Country.

Reprint Publishing

FOR PEOPLE WHO GO FOR ORIGINALS.

This book is a facsimile reprint of the original edition. The term refers to the facsimile with an original in size and design exactly matching simulation as photographic or scanned reproduction.

Facsimile editions offer us the chance to join in the library of historical, cultural and scientific history of mankind, and to rediscover.

The books of the facsimile edition may have marks, notations and other marginalia and pages with errors contained in the original volume. These traces of the past refers to the historical journey that has covered the book.

ISBN 978-3-95940-051-0

www.reprintpublishing.com

www.ingramcontent.com/pod-product-compliance
Lightning Source LLC
Chambersburg PA
CBHW071354170626
46811CB00003B/1127